INSIGHT PUBLICA

Nadakkave, Kozhikode, Kerala
Tel:0495–4020666
www.insightpublica.com
e-mail: insightpublica@gmail.com

Duffer's New Adventures
Aureliu Busuioc
Hubert And The Forbidden Frontier
Insight Publica Facsimile Edition: July 2020

ISBN 978-81-946829-5-0

Those fantastic Soviet Books Again

"All of us still have those fond memories of the books from the erstwhile Soviet Union, which were once extensively circulated here, in Kerala - books of fabulous tales, riveting scientific facts and enchanting illustrations which stole the readers' hearts. They left in us an indelible impression and an unforgettable reading experience. An experience still ever-green in us, Malayali diaspora.

As the Union got dissolved, those charming books of tales too vanished, turning them into cherished memories of nostalgia. Yet, readers have relentlessly been looking for those inimitable books. That was why we, the INSIGHT PUBLICA, published a few of them in the same mode. We are grateful and glad to say that readers whole-heartedly backed us in realizing the project.

During the execution of our mission, we could fathom the depth and breadth of a great nation's remarkable literary project. Those sublime Soviet stories traversed in translation into many a nation and many a language. Those books were ubiquitous-not as merchandise, but as products of culture.

The fantastic bolstering that INSIGHT PUBLICA could get is the impetus that drove us daringly to undertake the mission of reprinting and republishing those Soviet works in Indian languages.

You readers need not anymore be discontented with the scanned copies of these books. INSIGHT PUBLICA will help reach into your hands those very books with the same freshness and warmth.

Let us present you again those fantastic Soviet Stories with humility and pride."

Sumesh Insight

CONTENTS

Aureliu Busuioc

Duffer's new adventures

Translated from the Moldavian
by Dionisie Badarau

Illustrated by A. Khmelnitsky

DUFFER PLAYS
THE VIOLIN

Duffer received a violin as a present on his birthday.
It was from his grandmother.

«My darling,» she said, «a teacher of music will come to
you next week. He'll teach you to play and you'll become a
yreat musician.»

Some two days later, when Duffer's pains in the belly,
because of the cake he had eaten alone, abated, he remembered about the present. He took the violin in one hand
and the fiddlestick in the other, examining them attentively.

The violin smelled of lacquer, while the fiddlestick did
not smell of anything.

«Hm,» Duffer thought, «why is it necessary to engage a teacher for me? It's easy enough to play: if I want a low sound I pass the fiddlestick on the thickest string, if I want a high sound I choose the thinnest one!»

He put the violin under his chin.

«Well,» he said, «now I shall play... I shall play «Spring is coming, coming, coming!» One, two!»

He put the fiddlestick on the strings and pushed it as hard as he could.

«Squeak, squeak!» the violin played.

Vasilake, the cat, jumped down from the sofa and scampered into the kitchen.

The dog Bimbirel began to bark loudly.

«Shut up!» Duffer cried to him. «Don't you see that I have played the wrong string?"

He put the filddlestick on the thinnest string.

«Squeak, squeak!» the violin gave a higher sound.

«Oh... Probably the fiddlestick is not greased,» Duffer thought, and went to the kitchen, where Vasilake was trying to open the window and jump into the yard. He took some butter with a finger and spread it on the fiddlestick.

This time the violin did not play at all. Duffer did his best to make it play, but it was silent.

«Poor granny!» Duffer sighed. «They saw in the shop that she was not a good judge of musical instruments and gave her a broken violin... What am I to do not to sadden her?»

He threw the violin onto a corner of the sofa and lay down onto another one thinking.

An hour later he ran to the telephone.

«Granny, granny!» he cried in the receiver. «I have learned to play the violin! Myself! I don't need any teacher! Do you hear me? Come quickly to listen to me!»

Granny came in the afternoon. She had a big box of sweets in her hand. Uituchila and Googoolitsa were pattering in the room. Duffer put on his father's black coat, which was too wide for him, but he looked like a real musician.

«Well, let us listen to you, grandson,» granny smiled and sat down on the sofa. «It's a wonderful thing to learn to play the violin yourself!»

«Myself, myself!» shouted Duffer. «Is it so difficult after all? Here is the violin, here is the fiddlestick and here am I, the musician!» Duffer bowed down before granny to the ground.

«What would you like me to play?»

«Play what you know better,» granny said.

«Well?!» Duffer said gladly. «Then I shall play... I shall play «Waltz» by Tchukovsky.»

«Maybe Tchaikovsky?» granny corrected him.

«Oh, yes!»

Duffer made an unnoticed sign to Uituchila, who was sitting near the record-player, and raised the fiddlestick.

«Waltz. One, two!»

At first a wheezing was heard, then the melody began to sound: pim-pum-pum, trum-tum-tum...

Granny put on the glasses and looked attentively at the violin player. Duffer fervidly handled the fiddlestick.

ПОЗДРАВЛЯЕМ

«Uituchila, Googoolitsa!» granny said. «Why are you sitting there as if you were strangers? Come here close to me!»

Uituchila was so scatter-brained that he opened his mouth, while Googoolitsa made haste to granny and... fell down on the parquet.

The melody stopped stammering at once, while Duffer continued to play the violin but without producing any sound...

«Stop playing, Duffer!» Uituchila cried out. «Don't you see that the record does not wheel round? Googoolitsa has stumbled over the wire and the plug has come out of the socket!»

Granny stood up frowning.

«Good show, Duffer! Good show! Once more! A very nice concert! You are a great violin player!..» and she went out, taking the box of sweets she had come with.

In the evening father asked Duffer:

«Sonny, don't you happen to know who has greased my black coat with butter?..»

DUFFER GOES
SHOPPING

One day mother sent Duffer to the shop to buy some sunflower oil.

«But first you have to ask if it is good.»

Duffer took a bottle, took some money and went off. He walked for some time and soon came to the shop as it was nearby.

«Have you got sunflower oil?» he asked the shop assistant, forgetting to greet him.

«Yes, we have!»

«Is it good?»

«As good as honey!» the shop assistant answered in jest.

Duffer remained with his mouth open.

«If the sunflower oil is as good as honey,» he thought, «why not to buy honey?» And he went away.

He walked for some time and came to another shop.

«Have you got honey?»

«Yes, we have,» the shop assistant said, without answering Duffer's greeting, as the latter had not greeted him.

«And is it good?»

«As good as sugar?» the shop assistant answered in jest.

And again Duffer started to think and remained with his mouth open.

«Why should one take honey if sugar is also good?» he said and went away.

He walked for some time and came to another shop.

«Sugar!» Duffer said, while stepping the threshold.

«What? Sugar?» the shop assistant asked.

«Have you got it?»

«Yes, we have.»

«Is it good?»

«As good as fresh bread,» the shop assistant answered as he also was very facetious.

And Duffer returned from the threshold and went to the baker's.

«Have you got fresh bread?» he asked there.

«Have got what?» the baker laught.

«Bread,» Duffer said.

«Yes, we have,» the baker said.

«And is it good?»

«As good as milk!» the baker answered seriously, as he also was extremely facetious.

And again Duffer went away straight to the milk-man.

«Have you got milk?»

«Yes, we have.»

«Is it good?»

«As good as lemonade!» the shop assistant said, as he did not like milk.

Duffer turned at once and left the shop. He stopped near the stall where they sold lemonade.

«Have you got lemonade?» he asked.

«We have had, but we have run out of it just now,» the shop assistant said cheerfully.

Duffer remained with his mouth open and again began to think.

«If that's the case, I'll go home...»

He walked for some time and at last he came home.

«Well, Duffer,» mother asked him, «have you bought sunflower oil?»

«No, I haven't» he answered, «because they have run out of lemonade.»

DUFFER CATCHES
THE THIEF

Duffer came out of the house as he usually did: banging the door and jumping over three steps at a time. But he stumbled against the last step and came into the yard on his belly and with his nose scratched. He remembered that he had forgotten to take Bimbirel, the dog, with which he had to go for a walk.

«It's very nice that I have fallen,» Duffer said, as he never cried if nobody was there to see him falling. «It's very nice that I have fallen, as I have remembered Bimbi!»

He was rubbing his nose, which began to swell, becoming like a potato, and when he was just ready to return into the house, he noticed Uituchila, Googoolitsa, Mitica and some other friends at the bottom of the garden. All of them were standing quiet and none of them uttered a word. Duffer could not return into the house without finding out what had happened.

«Googoolitsa's cap has disappeared...» Mitica said. «Haven't you taken it, Duffer?»

Duffer wanted to give him a fillip, but then he remembered that Mitica went in for boxing and changed his mind.

«Where is my ca-a-a-p!.. Where is my ca-a-a-p!..» the looser began to shriek.

The fillip prepared for Mitica stopped on Googoolitsa's forehead.

«Shut up!» Duffer said. «Why are you bleating like a goat? What will you give me if I tell you where the cap is?»

«Where is it, where?» all of them cried.

«Where... where!..» Duffer teased them. «I don't know where, but I know how to find it.»

«How, how?» the children asked.

Duffer tried to frown but his nose began to burn even harder. So he made a serious face without frowning.

«Do you watch TV?»

«It's not in the TV se-e-t!» Googoolitsa whined. «Only father's fountain pen is there, but I am afraid to tell him about it...»

Duffer gave him another fillip.

«I ask if you watch television programmes. Films.»

«Y-e-e-s,» Googoolitsa said. «But I have never seen my cap there!»

«Then,» cried Duffer, looking proudly at his friends, «have you seen a film with a wolfhound, Akbar, which caught thieves?»

«Oh!» the children said. «Akbar!..»

«Not Akbar,» Duffer said still prouder. «Not Akbar, but Bimbirel! Wait for me here!»

Bimbirel was standing yelping near the door.

«Bimbi!» Duffer cried. «Be courageous and don't yelp! We both shall 'become very famous detectives. Come on!»

and, without waisting any time, he took the puppy into his arm and ran to the children.

All Duffer's friends were waiting impatiently.

«Well,» Uituchila said. «Googoolitsa's cap is four times bigger than Bimbirel!..»

«But Bimbi must not put it on,» said Mitica, «he must find the cap.»

«Oh, my ca-a-a-p! Oh, my ca-a-a-p!» Googoolitsa began to moan again.

«Don't howl!» Duffer cried to him. «Don't make Bimbirel nervous. Better give your head to him.»

«How can I give my head to him?» the small boy asked terrified.

«Bend so that he could smell you!» Mitica said. «Where is the puppy to know what you need?»

Googoolitsa bent down frightened out of his wits:

«And if he bites me?»

«Bimbi!» Duffer ordered. «Smell!»

Bimbirel began to lick Googoolitsa's forehead and hair.

«Now look for it!» Duffer ordered again. «Look for the cap!»

Bimbirel looked astonished at his master and wagged his tail.

«No, that won't do!» said Mitica. «Akbar smelled the thief's shoe, don't you remember? Googoolitsa, give your shoes to him!»

«I have no shoes, I have high galoshes on,» cried Googoolitsa.

«Then give your handkerchief to him,» Duffer said

severely. «Akbar found the girl who had got lost, after he had smelled her handkerchief.»

Googoolitsa took a crumpled handkerchief out of his pocket and held it out to Bimbirel.

It was just what the puppy seemed to have been waiting for. He took the crumpled handkerchief with the teeth and disappeared under the empty boxes thrown near the fence.

«Hurrah! Hurrah!» the children cried all together and started running after the courageous puppy.

«Your dog is better than Akbar!» said Uituchila.

Duffer was so proud that his ears began to grow bigger.

«Certainly he is better! He's a dog of a special breed.»

Bimbirel came out from under the boxes without any handkerchief and without any cap...

«M-y-y handkerchief!» Googoolitsa began, but, being afraid of Duffer's fillip, he stopped.

«Just a moment, just a moment!» said Mitica. «It seems to me that I understand something...» and he began to throw the boxes aside.

«Dear me!» Uituchila was the first to cry. «Here are my mittens, which I lost the day before yesterday!»

«And Lena's doll,» said Mitica.

«And my socks...» whispered Duffer.

«And my cap! Hurra-a-ah!» cried Googoolitsa.

There was a real storehouse under the boxes.

Everybody looked al Bimbirel and his master at once.

«Who may the thief be?» Uituchila asked.

Duffer took the puppy into his arms.

«Who may the thief be?» Googoolitsa asked too.

«Who?» Mitica amazed. «Let's guess! What do you say about it, Duffer?»

But Duffer could not answer because he was far away, going upstairs and jumping over three steps at a time with Bimbirel in his arms...

DUFFER REPAIRS
THE TV SET

One Sunday father called Duffer from the yard and told him:

«I have to go out with mother and Helen...»

«I want to go too!» Duffer grumbled.

«Oh, no,» said father. «Uncle Basil is to ring me up; you will have to present an apology on my behalf and tell him that I shall be back at four o'clock. Have you got it?»

«Yes, I have,» Duffer answered, extremely proud that father had so much confidence in him. «But will you switch on the TV set for me?»

«Certainly, certainly,» father said. «Well, but... have you understood?..»

There was a very interesting programme, a film about some children who were going for a motor run by a real car quite by themselves. Duffer was sitting on the sofa, laughing at the adventures of the prankish brats, and waiting for uncle Basil's telephone call.

But just when the car had to enter a dark forest full of mysteries, the TV set creaked for some time and the images disappeared from the screen.

«Well, well!» Duffer thought. «I know what you need, you capricious TV set! I'll do as father does!»

He rushed at the TV set and hit it with his fist on one side. The TV set was silent...

«It can't be otherwise,» Duffer thought. «Do I have as much power in my fist as father does?»

He went out into the corridor for father's dumb-bells. They were heavy but still he managed to raise them.

«Oh, no!» he thought.. «The film will be over before my muscles grow stronger!»

Then he came with the dumb-bells, aimed at the TV set and hit it from above.

The screen of the TV set became lighted and the voices were heard in a quick manner as if they were Uituchila when he intended to tell a lie.

«Hurrah!» Duffer cried. «Hurrah, I have repaired it! I am a great master! But... why isn't the film seen?»

Duffer turned all the buttons, hit the TV set with the dumb-bells again and again, but it would not work.

«Have a look at it!» the great mechanic said, scratching the back of his head. «It's playing the simpleton!»

Just at that moment the telephone rang.

«Uncle Basil, uncle Basil,» Duffer cried, without asking who was speaking. «Father has said to present his apology at four o'clock and to tell you that he will come on his behalf...» and he put down the receiver.

Hearing the key in the door, Duffer met his parents in the doorway.

«Father,» he said in a trembling voice. «I've seen a horrible film! Some naughty children got into a real car...»

«Has uncle Basil phoned?» father interrupted him.

«Yes,» Duffer said, «but when those mischievous children saw him, they got frightened and struck against the screen with the car... Just have a look at what has come out of them and their car.»

And he pointed at the heap of wires, buttons and broken valves lying under the TV set.

DUFFER HAS
A BAD LUCK DAY

It was raining, but it was an excellent day, the best one for sailing paper ships. But the grown-ups could not understand even such a thing. One had to sit in the house the whole day, look through the window how it was raining cats and dogs and a lot of rivers and seas were lost in vain...

Duffer had whimpered so much that at last mother took pity on him and let him go to Uituchila's to play.

«But be careful,» mother said, «take the umbrella and don't tread puddles!»

Duffer treaded puddles only halfway. From time to time he walked on the pavement as well. But then he remembered that he had not taken the umbrella...

«What am I to do?» he thought, making a wry face. «Am I to return home? If I return from my way it will mean that the things will take a bad turn with me for the whole day...»

He stopped in the middle of a stream thinking.

«Hurrah!» he cried at last. «I know what I shall do!»

He took Vasilake, the cat, out of his pocket and put him on his head.

«What a wonderful umbrella,» Duffer thought. «Nobody has such an umbrella.» But he did not manage to think it over better and yelled, «Vasilake bit him by the ear.»

«Oh, it means that you don't like the rain!» he cried. «Then learn to swim!» and he threw him just into the middle of the stream. «And still what am I to do? Am I to return home? I shan't be lucky...»

All at once he stood stone-still and gave a cry of surprise. Somebody had put a new basin under a drain pipe two steps from him to collect some rain water.

Duffer did not think too long: he poured out the water and put the basin on his head.

«Here, what a good umbrella I have!» he cried. «And it doesn't bite at all!»

His aunt, Uituchila's mother, opened the door.

«What have you come for, Duffer?»

«I've come to play with Uituchila.»

«And what have you brought the basin for?» she wondered.

«Well, the basin?» Duffer began to stammer out. «The basin?... The basin... Oh yes!.. Mother gave me the basin and asked you... Yes, she asked you to give her some flour!..»

The aunt stared at him, but he did not even bat an eyelid.

«All right,» the aunt said, «come in and play with your cousin, but be careful not to turn the house upside down.»

«O. K.!» Duffer said and ran into the room with the galoshes on.

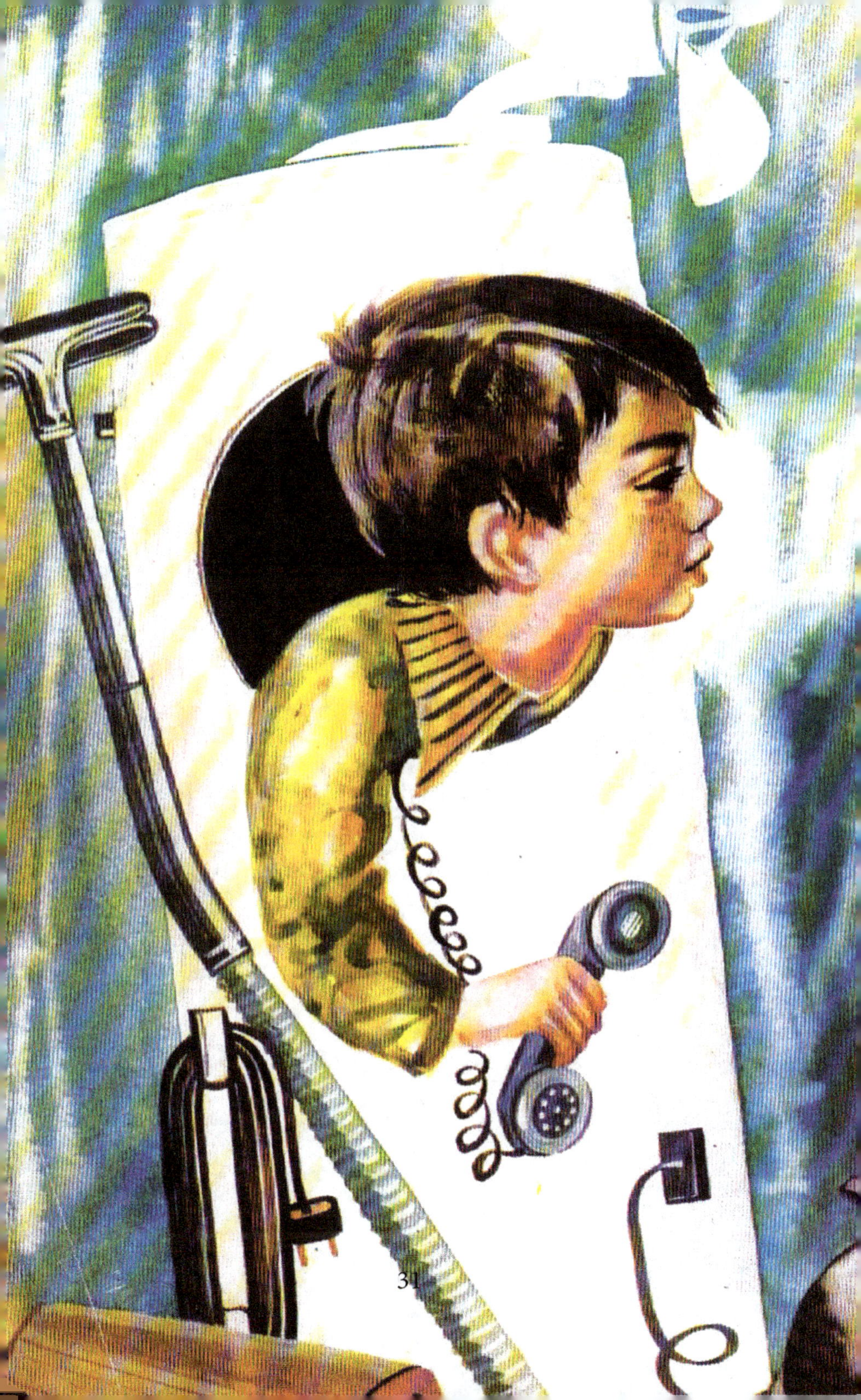

The cousins played very nicely, and broke only one vase, but nobody saw it, as they trew the fragments under the bed. Then Duffer took the basin and started for home. On his way he was thinking all the time of what to do with the flour: should he take it to mother or should he throw it away?...

But he had no time to take any decision: he approached the house from where he had taken the basin, and saw a little girl with an umbrella who had just come to the gate. Duffer took off the paper, which covered the flour, and put the basin under the drain pipe from which the water was gushing forth. Then he ran away.

He heard the high-pitched voice of the girl behind him:

«Mummy, mummy! Come quickly to see how it is raining dough!..»

In the evening, after he had stood in the corner for about two hours, Dufer was rubbing his red ears and thinking:

«Why have I had such a bad luck day today? I haven't returned home from my way to take the umbrella, have I?..»

DUFFER AND THE
TROUBLESOME NOSE

Uituchila, Googoolitsa and other children, whom Duffer had sent away from sleighing, began to make a snowman.

Duffer was waiting with great patience to have what to destroy.

The children had worked for rather a long time, but at last the snow bugaboo looked nice indeed. It had a pail with a lot of holes instead of cap, a broom under its armpit, coal eyes, and even a pipe in the mouth. But nobody had a carrot for nose.

Duffer was looking at that wonderful snowman, and was just ready to take a stick and destroy it, when he remembered that he had a doughnut in his hand, which he had been trying to eat for a whole hour. He ran up to the snow bugaboo and put it in the middle of the face instead of nose.

The children burst into laughter:

«Oh, have a look what a big nose this is,» Uituchilla said, «as if it were Duffer's nose!»

Duffer laughed too.

«My, what a big cap! It looks like Googoolitsa's cap!»

And while they were splitting with laughter, hop! the

cat Vasilake jumped out of Duffer's pocket, climbed up the snowman, took the doughnut and ran away.

The children were overdelighted. Only Duffer left for home crying.

«Mummy,» he hiccoughed. «Vasilake...»

«What has Vasilake done to you!» mother asked alarmed.

«Vasilake has eaten my nose...»

«Has it really happened as you say?» mother laughed. «And are you crying only because of that?»

«Why not to cry?» his sister Helen asked. «Where will he keep his fingers from now on?..»

DUFFER INVENTS
A NEW LANGUAGE

Duffer entered the house as red as a carrot because it was frosty and windy out of doors. Strictly speaking it was not so windy, he had been chasing Googoolitsa, the small cowardly neighbour with a snow ball.

«Mummy,» he cried from the threshold. «I am as hungry as a wolf. What will you gide me to eat?»

«Potato soup and macaronis with cheese, my darling!» mother said.

Duffer changed in the face and became as green as an unripe tomato but said nothing.

He walked to and fro in the room for some time, then stopped before mother:

«You know, mother, today we shall speak only the bird language!»

Mother laughed.

«Well, and how does this bird language sound? Just tell me something in it!»

«Cara mara bara!» squeaked Duffer.

«And what does it mean?»

«Guess!»

«I am not quite skilled at riddles,» mother said, «so go

and wash your hands and sit down at table.»

«Kiri miri biri,» Duffer answered.

«And what does this mean?» mother wondered.

«Cori mori bori!» he explained.

«Well, that's enough,» mother said. «Go to the table!»

«Kere mere, bere bere...» Duffer said again and lay on father's sofa.

Father and his sister Helen were waiting for him in the dining room.

«My darling, haven't you got a high temperature?» mother asked frightened, putting her hand on his forehead. «Haven't you eaten snow?»

«Chere mere vere,» Duffer sighed. «Vere mere chere!»

«Well. I don't like it,» mother frowned. «Aren't you ashamed to laugh at me in such a way?»

«Chocka bocka mocka!»

«That'll do! I'm angry with you! Will you come to table or not?»

Duffer wrinkled his face:

«Mocka bocka chocka! Bock bock...»

Mother got really angry and went out of the room: «You'll sit hungry all the day!»

Remaining alone Duffer began to think as he usually did.

What could he do if he liked neither potato soup nor macaronis with cheese? And nobody, absolutly nobody wanted to understand him...

Father entered the room:

«Pocka pocka pocka, Duffer! Hopa!»

«Lacka tacka!» Duffer answered.

«Have you really understood what I've said?» father
wondered.

«Ni-i...»

«I've said that a chiken roasted in sour cream is waiting
for us... Will it do?»

«It suits me!» Duffer jumped down from the sofa as a lion.

«Do you hear?» father cried. «Duffer has learnt our
language again!»

«And now,» father addressed him in the dining room,
«as you know how to speak our human language, be so kind
and eat potato soup and macaronis with cheese. And after
dinner you'll have to stand there in the corner, please. Is
it clear?..»

Since that day Duffer forgot the bird language and
began to like potato soup and macaronis with cheese
rather much...

HUBERT and
THE FORBIDDEN
FRONTIER

One day, Hubert decided to leave the city
for some time. He took his tent,
two blankets, his toiletry, a large sausage
and two bottles of lemonade.
Having reached the outskirts of a great forest,
he decided to set up his tent. Then, he lit
a fire and cooked half of his sausage,
after which he went to sleep.
The next morning, Hubert woke up
at sunrise. All was quiet in the woods.
On an oak tree, however, the finch chorale
was giving a concert, watched by a family
of blackbirds and two fox–cubs.
Under a fern-leaf, a snail was doing
his morning gymnastics. Three ants,
dragging a load of supplies for the anthill,
passed by shouting "Push-pull..."
On a bed of pine-needles, a grasshopper
and a frog were holding a jumping contest.
The referee was a very talkative mushroom.

Hubert ran to the brook to wash up.
The water was cool, and our friend was soon
well awake. He was so happy that he whistled
joyfully. A blackbird, puzzled at first
by the new song, soon joined in and they gave
such a marvellous concert that the frog
and the grasshopper stopped jumping,
the ants dropped their burden,
and the mushroom was silent.

Hubert then left
for a long walk in the forest.
He was happy, free, the air was cool.
He liked looking at the leaves glowing
with bright colours in the morning sun.
However, Hubert did not notice the little owl
following him from branch to branch.
He was much too busy watching a lark,
rising in the skies, singing.
Suddenly, the little owl gathered
courage enough to leave his hiding place
and approached Hubert, who was sitting
at the foot of a tree to take a rest.

"Little boy, would you listen to my story?"
"Speak, little owl".
"Well, I am very sad because, last night, a terrible battle was fought between crows and owls. We used to be friends, but, just after sundown, a crow flew over our territory in violation of our mutual agreement. Tonight, the council of the elders is meeting, and, if no one accepts to be a mediator, there will be war between crows and owls".

"I understand", Hubert exclaimed, "I have
an idea, I am coming with you."
And so, Hubert was seen following
the little owl leading the way to his territory.
A squirrel was so astonished that he almost
fell from his branch. As for the finch,
he choked with laughter.

That evening, the council of crows and owls
assembled. Hubert spoke: "Dear friends,
I know that men like to go to war,
but I did'nt realize that birds enjoyed
the same pastime. You are fighting for
so large a territory that you could never
possibly hinder each other. I want to submit

you an arrangement which I trust will satisfy
you. As owls work and play by night, while
crows prefer to stay awake in daytime, you could
very well share the same territory without ever
seeing or bothering each other. And so, the
forbidden frontier will no longer exist".

That same night a great feast was held
for the new friend of the birds. After the
customary speeches, in which owls and crows
thanked Hubert for having so wisely advised
them, the chief of the owls and the chief
of the crows advanced to the center of the
clearing, solemnly shook wings, swore to
eliminate the forbidden frontier and never
again to make war. Then, all rejoiced in a
magnificent banquet and wild dances.

The sun had already set when Hubert
returned to his tent. The little owl had come
too, and the two friends swore never to part.
Before going to sleep, Hubert remembered
his marvellous day, and decided to come back
and visit his forest friends every month.
He could do so, now that the forbidden
frontier was no more and that he was
everyone's friend.